SLOBCAT

Paul Geraghty

Macmillan Publishing Company   New York

Maxwell Macmillan International Publishing Group

New York   Oxford   Singapore   Sydney

For Harriet and the Moppets

Library of Congress Cataloging-in-Publication information is available.
ISBN 0-02-735825-9

Slobcat is our cat.
He does nothing but lie
around and sleep.

Heaven knows what
he does when we're
not there.

But when we get home he's
still sleeping. That's why
we call him Slobcat.

ERS 057-7462

When it's his supper time,
he's nowhere to be seen...

...and when we *do* find him,
he's even too lazy to eat.

I don't know *where* he goes
when we put him out…

...but he often comes back
all wet because he's
too lazy to get out of
the rain.

He spends so much
time inside...

…that he ends up getting in the way!

Last week Mom saw a
mouse, so Dad set
a trap...

…because Slobcat
isn't interested
in chasing mice.

All *he's* interested in is lying about
in the sun.

Luckily,
we don't have rats...

…because if we did,
Dad says we'd have to
get a *real* cat.

Some people have
dangerous animals
in their gardens.

But for some reason,
they don't seem to
come into ours.

It's strange because
the *little* creatures
don't seem afraid.

Sometimes, when we're asleep, there are burglars around.

Thank goodness
we have Brutus to
frighten them
off…

...because Slobcat couldn't frighten a flea!

People say that all cats have a secret
life that we don't know about…

...but I'm sure Slobcat's much too lazy for that!